THE NAMELESS

by Chad Mooney

DORRANCE
PUBLISHING CO
EST. 1920
PITTSBURGH, PENNSYLVANIA 15238

Dorrance Publishing Co
585 Alpha Drive
Suite 103
Pittsburgh, PA 15238
Visit our website at *www.dorrancebookstore.com*

ISBN: 978-1-6495-7170-0
eISBN: 978-1-6495-7679-8

THE NAMELESS

Misery is manifold. The wretchedness of earth is multiform. Overreaching the wide horizon as the rainbow, its hues are as various as the hues of that arch—as distinct, too, yet as intimately blended. Overreaching the wide horizon as the rainbow! How is it that from beauty I have derived a type of unloveliness?—from the covenant of peace a simile of sorrow? But as, in ethics, evil is a consequence of good, so, in fact, out of joy is sorrow born. Either the memory of past bliss is the anguish of to-day, or the agonies which *are* have their origin in the ecstasies which *might have been.*

—"Berenice," by Edgar Allan Poe

Some of the more graphic details of these stories may be difficult for the fainter of heart and the weaker of stomach to properly digest, but they are, after all, true stories, and worth noting, if only as a historic record of events transpired.

OBJECT PERMANENCE

Upon focusing my gaze upward I see above me a cloudless night sky devoid of any of the light pollution that one must contend with when staring up at city skies, a vast canopy filled with millions of tiny pinprick holes where the long-forgotten dead could peer down upon our tragic little soap opera lives as they unfolded into inevitability far below them in Technicolor-drenched Dolby 5.1 1080p real-time—surveying all the damage that we do—and where the brilliant glint of the angels above us shone through. And it all seemed to sway about slowly and somewhat fluidly—like through soft water—so that *every hole in the sky* appeared brimming so full of whatever perfect cosmic energy it is that they possess that they simply *could not be still.*

The stars, that is. The mescaline makes them all uneasy.

And, as I often do during these intensely introspective moments, I reflect, and I find myself thinking of her, and I can't help but wonder if she is looking up at these exact same stars in this exact same moment in space and time as well, and, more importantly to me, if she is, does she view them the same way that I do?—as monstrous spheres of heated gas which will eventually explode fantastically as terrifyingly destructive supernovae—or does she instead view them wondrously and in a decidedly less-apocalyptic fashion, like through the eyes of a small child?

Neither would really surprise me.

In those days in which we both dwelled upon the same closed plane, had I been a man of a more self-assured and confident nature, I'd have simply asked her myself—just strode right up to her in a casual-yet-purposeful way and struck up a random conversation with her, dazzling her in the process with my imagined wit and charm, my intelligence and sophistication, all the while making the requisite amount of eye contact and smiling at her in a non-threatening way at appropriate intervals—but alas, as this was not the case, I chose instead to simply admire her from afar.

Her name was Kellie with an "I-E"; I knew this not because we had ever spoken to one another, and not because I had overheard others speaking about her, but because one day, after weeks of watching her from my window, feeling quite emboldened, I finally seized initiative and stole some of her mail. More specifically, I stole a BJ's coupon book, a water bill, and a *Cosmopolitan* magazine. I had no use for the BJ's coupon book, as I am not a BJ's Club Member, nor for the water bill, so I managed to secret these items back into her mailbox without anyone noticing or becoming suspicious, but I opted to keep the *Cosmopolitan* magazine. Of course, it was not lost on me that, for the more confident and self-assured man, this magazine would have served as a kind of golden ticket of sorts, the perfect opportunity for an ice-breaking that would have opened the door for not only an introduction but perhaps even an ongoing dialogue had I simply knocked on her door and hand delivered the magazine to her myself. "Well, hello there. I believe *this* belongs to you; the mailman must've placed it into my mailbox by mistake. By the way, my name is . . . ."

But by then, I was already entrenched in my own mind too deeply—I had already built her up into goddess-like status, something utterly unattainable for someone like me—an unrequited dream—and I tended to act accordingly. This wasn't so much self-depreciation as it was a simple learned response based upon nearly every interaction I'd ever had with virtually every beautiful woman I have ever encountered, and it was deeply ingrained in me, rooted well below the surface of my psyche, a seed planted by my mother and cultivated by all the others along the way. Just like all the beautiful women in that *Cosmopolitan* magazine would have surely done, she would have certainly rejected me, and that rejection (and the festering wound it would have caused me) would have been a far worse thing for me to bear than the longing and the loneliness I would ultimately choose to reside within.

Here and now, in this very moment in space and time, staring up at the multitude of stars which blanket the sky around a waning crescent moon, the low-grade mescaline I've ingested making them all appear much closer than they actually are, I can vividly remember the first time I ever saw her: It was during that in-between time of year— not quite summer anymore, yet not quite yet autumn—and she was running recreationally around the block, her long, brilliantly colored vermillion-hued hair pulled back into a ponytail which swayed left to right like a pendulum as her tiny feet pounded the pavement like a metronome keeping perfect time with my heartbeat, her bare arms pumping like pistons back and forth, her long legs striding to keep pace with the dog that accompanied her. I could easily tell it was of the Rottweiler breed; its name, however, I never learned, nor did I particularly care to find out, as I've never really been what many people annoyingly refer to themselves as "a dog person."

Quite the opposite, in fact.

And, as I watched her run past my house time and time again with that drooling brute by her side, I came to the realization that she was something that I needed very badly to be close to, in one way or another—it was a revelation of an almost cosmic nature, fueled by simple physics and complex chemical reactions—an unseen force pulling me toward her like gravity, a kind of hopeful hopelessness, a reticent confidence in the genesis of an unbreakable covalent bond—though I knew my innate reserve would severely hinder such a bold and wistful endeavor.

So I continued to watch her in secret, mostly from the safety of my own living room, other times from the front yard under the guise of doing yardwork when I knew she would likely be running past—mowing the grass or raking the leaves while listening to Oasis on repeat through my headphones, a band I imagined she'd enjoy listening to very much, singing along with the lyric *maybe you're the same as me, we see things they'll never see, you and I are gonna live forever* despite the fact that I cannot hit the high note. And I even began jogging around the block myself—never at the same time in which she was running, of course—even going so far as to buy myself running shoes and other appropriate attire to look the part—not so much for the exercise, of course, but for the chance to view her house up close and personal as I jogged past, usually in the evening time when her living room light was on and I could see inside her house from the road. And, as time went on and the sun dropped from the sky earlier and earlier I became bolder and bolder, jogging later and later, eventually even creeping up to her windows under the cover the darkness, particularly during the new moon phase of the month when the night was at its blackest, and peering into those windows the times when the dog wasn't inside the house to bark at me; she tended to release him into the fenced in backyard quite frequently. And it eventually became a game of sorts, me trying to catch a secretive glimpse of her through the window and the dog trying to alert her to my presence from behind the fence those times when it wasn't inside the house with her.

This continued on for the better part of the fall, not every day or even every week, but regularly enough to where the dog became familiar with my scent when it was in the backyard and I was at the side window and began to look for me at the windows whenever it was inside the house, and its barking increased along with my frustration. It had gotten to the point for me where simply *seeing* her wasn't enough anymore—I needed to *feel* her, even if only by extension, which meant that I needed to get inside that house somehow, perhaps take a souvenir of sorts that I could touch and smell—I was leaning heavily toward a pair of her panties—but I knew this would be impossible given the virtual omnipresence of the dog. So, I made what seemed to me to be the only logical decision I could make under the circumstances: I had to get rid of the dog.

So I bought a pack of three steaks—nice center-cut filets, a good eight ounces apiece—and some latex gloves and a box of rat poison, acquiring all three items at different stores around the area, and I heavily dusted the filets with the rat poison and fed them to the dog by tossing them over the fence when I knew it was back there. After that, I never saw the dog again.

I also noted, interestingly enough, that she stopped running after that as well.

Three days later, when I was sure that she was at work doing whatever it was that she did during the workday, concealing a crowbar as best I could up my sleeve, I slipped into her backyard with the intention of breaking in through the rear sliding-glass door. I saw there in the yard a fresh mound of dirt and instantly knew I was looking at the dog's grave; I also knew that I should have felt some remorse for taking away from her something that she had loved so much and had shared so many moments with, created so many memories with—for causing her even a modicum of pain—but it was simply something that needed to be done—collateral damage, as it were—and I was more preoccupied with getting into the house than with feeling any feelings other than the electric nervous excitement I was experiencing.

As it turned out, I needn't have brought the crowbar—to my shock and surprise, the sliding-glass door was unlocked. I smiled darkly to myself and disappeared silently inside.

Stepping into the house was like slipping into a warm bath of scented water; her heat was on, set at a balmy seventy-eight degrees, according to the thermostat on the wall, and the first thing I noticed was the bright-red color she'd painted the walls—it basically matched the color of her hair—but what really caught my attention was the smell. It smelled just like I'd imagined inside the house, a lot like that *Cosmopolitan* magazine with all its perfume samples. I immediately busied myself going about the house and smelling everything—her unlit candles, her perfumes and lotions, her clothes, the soap and shampoo in her shower, her pillows and bedsheets, everything. I couldn't get enough.

I spent about a half-hour in the house, looking around and smelling things, and feeling soft things such as fabrics against the smoothness of my cheek and the pads of my fingertips (I couldn't help but take the latex gloves off) just for the many sensations they gave me, and I laid in her unmade bed and closed my eyes, seeing her colors swirling on the back of my eyelids, imagining she was lying there curled up beside me, her hair draped softly across the pillow. After experiencing these things, I was careful to put everything back exactly as I had found it so as not to alert her to the fact that anyone was in the house.

Of course, had I needed to use that crowbar to gain access to the house, I would never have been able to take off those gloves.

Later that night, I crept up to her window and I watched her watch TV. She sat sideways in her recliner, her pajama-clad legs slung over the armrest, her right hand holding the remote control, her arm snaking out sporadically to change the channel, and I remained there longer than I ever had before, watching her until well after she fell asleep, seemingly at peace, and I imagined living within the confines of a completely different world, a world in which she could belong to me, a world in which we took long walks together and held hands, a world in which her body was mine for the taking, a world in which she gave it up to me freely and longed for the touch of my own flesh as well, a world in which anything was possible.

It would be the last time I would ever see her; she moved away from the neighborhood two days later.

Here and now, looking back with 20/20 hindsight and a head full of mescaline, I assume it had a lot to do with someone poisoning her dog. I lock eyes with Sirius, the brightest star in our sky, which is actually two stars, a binary system consisting of a main-sequence star twice the size of our sun (Sirius A), which will one day go supernova, and a white dwarf star (Sirius B), which will eventually just fade away and die, orbiting around each other at a period of about every fifty years or so, and I wonder where Kellie went, where she is now. Maybe close by; maybe oceans away.

Perhaps our orbits will have us crossing paths again someday.

At any rate, in as far as killing the dog so that I may enter her home and acquire for myself a souvenir was concerned, I needed not commit the act at all, as it turned out.

There wasn't a single pair of panties in the entire house, and I left there empty-handed.

SOMEWHERE BETWEEN
SCREAMING AND CRYING

[1.1]

"You still act like you."

My wife says this tonelessly to me as she's driving down the road a bit faster than she probably should be, the hospital growing smaller and smaller in the rearview mirrors, the summer sun shining down hot and unimpeded by the sparsely-spaced clouds high above us. It's bright out; I'm wishing I had a pair of sunglasses to hide my eyes behind. The car radio is on at a high-volume—the neurologist had said that playing my favorite music might help trigger my memory—and my wife had gotten excited when a particular song had come on ("Oooh, this is our song!" she'd exclaimed), turning up the volume and singing along with it while glancing at me expectantly:

I don't care if it hurts, I want to have control, I want a perfect body, I want a perfect soul, I want you to notice when I'm not around . . .

and though the song was vaguely familiar to me, it didn't bring back any flooding memories or other familiar feelings of any kind, and she seemed more than a little disappointed.

You still act like you. Her words hang like counterweights in my head.

9

"What do you mean?" I ask her after a fashion, while staring out the window at a completely unfamiliar world as it glides by me just beyond the glass barrier.

"Your mannerisms—" says this completely unfamiliar woman with whom I'm to share the rest of my life with, "they're still the same. You still act like *you*."

I take this in as she swings the car around an onramp to the highway and accelerates to speed. "Well, that's . . . *good*," I finally say, trailing off a bit. "That's encouraging."

I don't really know what else to say or do so I simply focus my gaze upon the rapidly passing asphalt directly in front of the car, and then, on the grass alongside the edge of the highway. In vehicles all around us, people are living out their lives and going on about their business, most of them with no more understanding of themselves and their own place within the world than I currently possess about my own self, and for some reason, this isn't as comforting to me as it probably should be. My wife is quiet for a minute or two, allowing the song to play out and another to instantly take its place before muting the volume on the radio and turning slightly toward me in her seat, and she takes off her sunglasses, her big blue eyes darting quickly between me and the highway out in front of her.

She takes in a deep breath and sighs audibly, clears her throat and begins speaking; I can tell from her tone and the measured way in which she chooses her words that this is something she has been meaning to say for some time now.

It almost seems rehearsed.

"Look—I can't even *begin* to imagine what this must be like for you, going to live with what amounts to be a complete stranger like this. I know it must be hard for you, and probably even a little scary. But try to understand, it's hard for *me* too. We *have* to be able to talk to one another." She pauses, allowing this to sink in. I say nothing;

I'm not even looking at her. Undaunted, she continues, pushing through. "I mean, there's *got* to be things you want to know. Isn't there anything you'd like to ask me?"

I'm at a loss. How do I not own a pair of sunglasses?

"Like what?" I ask helplessly.

"*Well—I—don't—know*," she begins, maybe a little annoyed, maybe just trying to be patient with me, "like maybe you have questions about me. You know, so that you can get to know me a little better? I mean, we *do* share a life and a home together—it might make things easier if you knew more about me. I already know all about you."

I had considered this. I know intellectually that I have both a physical as well as an emotional history with this woman—and yet, she stands a stranger to me. All I really know about her is her name and the fact that we've been married for nine years, without children, and that, for some reason I may never understand, she's maddeningly in love with me.

I had also considered not going home with her at all—like maybe getting a hotel room for the time being instead—but I was less than optimistic about my chances of surviving all on my own with no memory. And I *did* have questions, lots of them, I just wasn't sure how to ask them. I steal a sideways glance at her; she's really very pretty; I can see why I married her. She notices me looking at her the way I'm looking at her and tucks a stray strand of brunette hair behind her ear to better show me her face and smiles knowingly. Outside the car, it's a skin-melting one-hundred-and-one degrees, according to the little display on the dash; inside the car, it's freezing.

"Well?" she finally asks me. "Anything at all?"

I stall for time, pretend to look at a man changing a flat tire on the shoulder as we speed past. She glances over at me.

"I'm trying to think of something," I say feebly.

She sighs again. As I'm thinking, the seconds of silence tick away like atomic bomb blasts between us inside my head.

[1.2]

Ten patient minutes later my wife has explained to me that her favorite color is periwinkle blue and that her favorite hobby is reading about and watching shows about true crime stories, and that she works in an administrative capacity in the same hospital I was just a patient in—among many other superficial things—but I'm still no closer to actually getting to know her than I was ten minutes ago. I can tell she's somewhat frustrated by the questions I'm asking (or, more likely, *not* asking) but she hides it fairly well.

"This is fun," she'd actually said at one point, maybe sarcastically, maybe not, as I asked her question after meaningless question about herself, "it's kind of like a first date." I was assuming she was referring to the awkwardness of it all and I agreed with her, and we actually shared a laugh together, our first. And then, before I know it, she's aiming the car toward an exit ramp and leaving the highway, and I know we're nearing "home" and I'm feeling a quiet uneasiness that I'm sure she can probably sense, though she says nothing. Finally, I work up the courage to ask her a real question.

"So, where am I going to sleep?"

She takes pause, taken aback, maybe even frowns a little—it's hard to tell in the glare of the sun. She squints against it, sunglasses still off, and she speaks to me slowly and carefully, as if explaining something sensitive to a small child. "Well, I was assuming you'd sleep with *me*, in *our* bed," she says, maybe a little angry, maybe a little hurt, "but if you'd be more comfortable sleeping in the spare room for the time being, then by all means, you're welcome to it. I certainly don't want you to be uncomfortable." She pauses again, looking straight ahead, clears her throat again. "It's *your* house too, you know," she adds, a slight bite detectable in her voice.

I say nothing, merely nod my head slowly. Outside the car, main roads give way to side roads and I find myself thinking about how far away the hospital is right now, maybe wishing I was still there. She turns the radio back up, another vaguely familiar song that brings no familiarity along with it, and I'm trying to think of something nice to say to her but nothing really comes to mind. Staring out the window, I see nice middle-class houses with well-manicured yards of green grass and shade trees standing in mulch beds, squarely trimmed hedges and privacy fences—a true Norman Rockwell portrait of the American Dream—and after a minute or two of winding our way down and along roads that I'm afraid I'm never going to learn to negotiate and navigate all on my own, my wife turns off the road and pulls into a driveway leading up to a house not unlike all the other houses which stand along the same street in the neighborhood I now call "home."

"Here we are," she says cheerfully, putting on a brave new face, and I'm thinking to myself, *Don't say it, please don't say it*, and then she says it and I cringe a little inside, "Home sweet home!"

She brings the car to a stop and puts it in park, turns fully toward me in her seat and looks at me eagerly, asks me if anything looks familiar. There's a silver Dodge Ram 1500 in the driveway (I assume it's mine) and an American flag swaying gently in an almost nonexistent breeze as it hangs from a pole on the front porch. The street address is 1428; it's posted on the mailbox and again in big brass numbers on the porch column where the flag is hanging from. There are pristinely cut hedges beneath the windows and a freshly mown lawn which all frame the house nicely—we obviously have a professional lawn service—and a privacy fence wrapped around the backyard.

None of it looks very familiar to me.

"Well?" she asks. "Anything registering?"

"Not *really*," I say slowly, as if I had to think about it first.

Already, I hate disappointing her.

"Don't worry," she says, taking my hand in hers and squeezing it until I squeeze back, "we'll get through this together. It'll all come back to you; it just might take some time. In the meantime . . . ." She leans over across the cab and kisses my cheek; it feels nice. She makes a face. "The first thing you need to do is *shave*," she says, in reference to the beard I have developed over the last few weeks in the hospital.

I rub my jawline tentatively. "I don't know," I say finally, "I kind of like it."

Sitting this close, I can smell the lotion she uses on her skin, her shampooed hair.

"Come on," she says excitedly, fairly pushing me out of the car, "I'll show you around the castle, my prince."

After being in that freezing car, it feels like being pushed headfirst into an oven.

[2.1]

Walking into the house feels like entering an unfamiliar room in someone else's house without their permission, a room you know you shouldn't be going into but you decide to press on anyway. Once inside, my wife whisks me from room to spotless room, taking special care to show me pictures of the two of us smiling and embracing in various settings, as if proving a point, but none of them seem to register with me—they might as well be the stock portraits that come in picture frames when you buy them at the store. The décor is tasteful-yet-minimal, the furniture mostly black leather, the tables, chairs and bookshelves made of nice wood. The flooring is all ceramic tile or wood planks, depending upon the room you're in—there is no carpet, and very few rugs. Everything is perfectly clean and meticulously organized—even the books on the bookshelf are arranged in alphabetical order by the author's last name. Also, there's a dog bed and a basket of chew toys in the living room but no dog.

"Where's the dog?" I ask. Her eyes light up instantaneously.

"*Oh!*—you remember Rambo!" she gushes, clasping her hands together.

Again, I hate to disappoint her.

"*No,*" I say slowly, choosing my words carefully so as not to upset her again, "it's just that I see dog stuff but there's no dog. Where is it?"

Her face falls a little, the light momentarily leaving her eyes, but she recovers quickly and reapplies her bubbly façade. "Oh. Well. *He* is at Mike and Laura's house; they're friends of ours; they live just down the street. They've been taking care of him for us while we've been at the hospital." She pauses, looks at me. "You'll like them. We're all having dinner together tomorrow night." She's being so nice to me that I do my best to hide my displeasure at the prospect of re-meeting people. She continues talking. "And anyway, Doctor Roberts said it's important for you to surround yourself with familiar people—it might help jog your memory. And since neither of us have any family . . . ."

She stops speaking, looks at me as if she'd just inadvertently shared a forbidden secret. This, of course, does nothing but pique my interest. "What happened to our families?" I ask.

She looks so sad explaining, I almost regret asking her in the first place. She gives me the CliffsNotes version, glossing over it fairly quickly. "You were an only child; your father left when you were born and you never met him; your mother never remarried and died in a car accident when you were twenty. I was adopted by an older-than-usual couple who were unable to have children of their own; they died within a few months of each other two years ago."

Uncomfortable silence. "I'm sorry," I find myself saying, though I don't know for whom and I'm not sure why.

She looks at me warmly, eyes watery, continues on. "Anyway, Mike and Laura are our best friends." She pauses again, wipes her eyes carefully with an index finger so as not to ruin her makeup. "You really don't have many friends, you know."

I say nothing. She continues to look at me, making certain that I have fully understood the vital importance of meeting with such good friends of ours that I apparently like so much, and then, slowly, a mischievous little smile curls the corners of her mouth slightly upward; it's hardly perceptible, but it's there if you're looking closely enough. "Come on," she says, pulling me by the arm, "the bedroom is this way." And before I can mount a protest of any kind, she's practically dragging me down a hallway (more pictures on the walls, some of her and I, some of some other people I do not recognize, some with a chocolate lab I can only guess is Rambo) and I'm pleasantly surprised to find that it smells vaguely familiar to me, though I can't place exactly how or why. She opens a door, flips on a light.

"Here it is," she says, gesturing grandly with one arm while clinging to one of mine with the other, "this is where the magic happens." I look at her. She winks, smiles somewhat dirtily at me; I feel myself blush, but only slightly.

I'm hoping she doesn't register my embarrassment.

I turn my attention to the bedroom. *The bed is enormous*, I'm thinking—it takes up most of the room. There's another dog bed at the foot of it and a large flat-screen TV hanging on the bedroom wall opposite the headboard. There are bedside tables with lamps on either side of the bed, and a long wooden dresser along the interior wall.

There's a walk-in closet. It's all very neat and clean.

All of it seems distantly familiar to me, like something I've seen in a dream, that odd feeling of déjà vu.

"It smells . . . *familiar*," I say, oddly proud to report this to her.

"Good," she purrs, pulling me close while tilting her head back to kiss me on the lips for the first time. I kiss back. It feels nice. "Maybe it won't be long before you start remembering things," she adds.

"Hopefully," I say, blood flowing to my groin area from the kiss. I can feel myself blushing again—this time I'm sure she notices.

She looks up into my eyes. "I'm just so glad you're home," she coos, hugging me tightly. I wrap my arms around her, hugging her back. She's very warm and soft, and her hair smells like flowers. "*Now*—" she begins, shifting gears to upbeat as she pulls away from me, "*there's* the bathroom. Your clothes are in the dresser and hanging in the closet, towels are in the bathroom closet, and everything you need to wash the hospital off of you is on the rack in the shower. You go get cleaned up; I'll be in the kitchen making dinner. I'm making your favorite tonight." She squeezes my hand, lets go.

"What is it?" I ask.

"What is what?" she wants to know.

"My favorite dinner. What is it?"

She smiles playfully. "It's a surprise," she says coyly, poking me in my stomach with a bony little index finger. "I just hope you're hungry."

I assure her that I am. She leaves me standing there in the bedroom and walks out the door and down the hallway; I find myself watching her walk away until she disappears around the corner, her pheromones still fresh in the air all around me. After she moves out of view I find my attention shifting toward a wedding photo of the two of us smiling and embracing on the wall above the headboard. I stare into my own dancing eyes; I look genuinely happy.

Being unable to remember it, it makes me feel strange.

[2.2]

In the shower I'm making a mental list, thinking about all the things I do and do not know.

Facts I know to be true: I had viral encephalitis, I went into a coma from the fever, I awoke with retrograde amnesia due to damage to my amygdala. Things unknown: how I met my m wife, how to do my job, how we celebrate the holidays. Fact: I own a dog most likely named after a beloved Sylvester Stallone character. Unknown: just how many dogs I've owned over my thirty-six years on this planet—all those close connections suddenly severed by the encephalitis. It's the same with all the people I've ever known as well—although the lost connections with all those people don't bother me near as much as the lost connections with all those dogs, which leads me to other epiphanies about myself concerning my relationships with human beings.

After thoroughly washing my hair and body I stand there in the shower for a long time and allow the water to run over me; as the hot water gradually cools, I turn the temperature knob by tiny degrees, hotter and hotter, in order to maintain a comfortable water temp, until the hot water finally runs out completely and I'm forced to turn off the water and face the world again.

When I finish drying off I stand there in front of the mirror and I take a good, long, hard look at myself. My eyes are piercing blue but there doesn't seem to be anything behind them—they seem almost empty as I stare into them. My beard has yet to be trained. I can tell that I normally keep my hair short because, even after weeks of growth, it isn't very long. Maybe it just grows slowly. I look at my body. I'm fit but not muscular (though I probably lost some significant weight in the hospital), tall but not towering, tan but not bronzed, decent-looking but not overtly handsome. In other words, I'm your everyday slightly-above-average thirty-six-year-old everyman who can tell you how many games the Jacksonville Jaguars won last year but not about the first time he saw his wife naked.

Before getting dressed, I practice smiling at myself in the mirror.

After a minute or two, I feel as though I've gotten pretty good at it.

I open four dresser drawers before I find the one with men's boxer shorts in it; I open all of them before I realize my wife hangs up my pants in the closet along with my shirts. Once dressed, I take the bedroom doorknob in my hand and I pause, taking in a nice, deep breath before swinging open the door and striding boldly down the hallway toward the kitchen.

The scent of seafood cooking hits my nostrils immediately. Music wafts to my ears from the kitchen, a song I do not recognize. As I enter the kitchen, I see my wife with her back to me, bending down and over into the refrigerator. I admire her buttocks, her naked feet, and I'm thinking to myself, *She has a great body*. She stands back upright, turns to face me, and, smiling brightly, holds out a bottle of beer toward me while holding a bottle of Moscato in the other hand. I take the beer from her while flashing my best megawatt smile at her; her own smile grows even bigger and brighter, her eyes glinting at me.

"Feeling better?" she asks. I nod as I crack open the beer and take a swig. She moves over to the oven, places the Moscato on the counter and slides on an oven mitt, pulls open the oven door. She then pulls out the middle rack with her gloved hand and proceeds to baste two large lobster tails with melted butter before sliding the rack back in and closing the oven door.

"I've got lobster tails, shrimp, fried rice and mashed potatoes going," she says to me above the music, pointing to various pots and pans simmering on the stove. "It'll all be ready soon."

"It smells really good," I say, taking another sip of beer. She winks at me before pouring herself a glass of the Moscato and I'm about to ask her about the song that's playing because I like it, when, all of a sudden, as if activated into existence by my voice, a large brown flash comes tearing into the kitchen and leaps up into my groin. I buckle slightly, cursing under my breath, unsure of what is happening, before quickly regaining my composure. I then get my free hand on the creature leaping happily at my feet and attempt to control its jumping. "This must be Rambo," I say while rubbing the dog's head. It licks my hand.

My wife gushes. "He's so happy to see you!" She walks over and bends down at the waist to pet the dog along with me, kisses it on top of the head. "Did you miss your daddy?" she asks the dog. "I wanted you to be surprised," she tells me, straightening up and looking at me. "I went and got him real quick while you were taking your marathon shower."

I look down at the dog looking up at me smiling. I look at my wife looking at me smiling.

Both of them seem genuinely happy in this moment.

I can feel myself warming up to it.

And a voice is coming from the speaker, singing *every new beginning comes from some other beginning's end . . . .*

And just like that, my new beginning has begun, and my brand-new ready-made family is complete.

[2.3]

Dinner begins as an awkward exercise in the two of us trying to get reacquainted, and I'm remembering the comment my wife made earlier about it being like a first date but it isn't really, because there is the very real pressure of keeping a marriage going hanging over our heads like a massive grey raincloud bloated big with doubt and uncertainty, and we're either trying too hard to force things or simply not trying hard enough—it's hard to tell which is the case. I'm alternately silent and noncommittal and cautiously reticent; my wife is alternately optimistically cheerful and gently pressing and ultimately frustrated. Finally, during another long and relatively uncomfortable lull in the conversation, I put down my fork and look at her.

"So tell me—what was I like before?"

She smiles thoughtfully and maybe somewhat sadly, her big blue eyes going far away, as if looking into a distant past. "You were always sweet, and funny. You always made me laugh. And *so* smart. You read a lot of different books about a lot of different things—you had varied interests—and you used to help me with my crossword puzzles. You just knew the answers. Except of course for the pop culture clues; you never had any interest in that. But you were also very private at times—you liked to drive around a lot, especially at night, just to get away and center yourself." She pauses, chuckles to herself, continues to speak about me as though I were dead, as if giving a eulogy. "But you were always very loving toward me, very touchy-feely." She stops talking and looks down at her plate, as if some answer were hidden there, stirs her fork into her mashed potatoes. "I fell in love with you very quickly."

"And now?" I ask tentatively, holding my breath, the question hanging uncertainly in the air between us.

She sighs, not really looking at me. "And now . . . you're not yourself." She shrugs and spears a piece of lobster with her fork, puts it into her mouth and chews thoughtfully. "*But* . . . ," she continues, that upbeat, always-sunny and optimistic disposition returning to her face and voice, "Doctor Roberts said that was to be expected. Your personality should return along with your memory. And I have faith that it will."

I'm quiet for a moment, staring at my own plate of food, looking for something that cannot be found. "Why?" I finally ask her.

"Why? Why what?"

"Why do you have faith?"

"Because," she says, looking at me lovingly, as if I were a child asking an innocuous question, "faith is all that I have."

This is followed by a long and penetrating silence that I feel compelled to break, with anything at all. "*Sooo*—" I begin, my mind grasping for something to say, "how exactly did I get sick in the first place?"

She takes a sip of her Moscato, her lip gloss leaving a clear smudge on the rim of the wine glass. "It started out as a viral infection," she says. "They told us at the hospital it had developed into encephalitis. You had a one-oh-six-point-something degree fever; it literally fried your brain and put you into a coma. When you finally woke up, your memory was gone. You had no idea who I was. I cried and cried." She falters slightly, looks at me sadly before smiling that same warm smile I've become so accustomed to seeing on her face. "But here you are." She takes my hand from across the table and squeezes it; I squeeze back. Her eyes begin to water; I feel a sudden need to change the subject.

"Well—" I say, before finishing my beer and dropping her hand so that I can get up from the table and retrieve another bottle from the refrigerator, "I have to hear the story. How did we meet? Please tell me it was ridiculously romantic."

She laughs out loud as I crack open my beer and sit back down at the table across from her, dabs her eyes with a napkin and begins speaking. And as she's speaking, something strange happens: as I'm listening to her tell the story of how she rear-ended me in a parking lot, my brain begins sparking recognition and I start to remember the *story*—I just don't remember the actual moment itself, not yet. I know the story because I've told it myself countless times, but I cannot quite seem to picture it happening in my mind because *this* me wasn't there to see it—the *other* me was.

I listen to my wife tell the story. ". . . and the strange thing to me, at the time—because it was totally my fault—was that you weren't even mad. Like, at all. You were just so calm and laid back about the whole thing, like you always are about everything. I wasn't expecting that. Of course, now I'm used to it. Anyway, my license had been expired for a few days and I didn't want to get the cops involved so we just exchanged information and drove off on our separate ways, and I thought that was that, but then—"

"Then I called you two days later," I find myself saying almost robotically, "and I told you I thought you owed me dinner for busting up my truck."

Her eyes flutter like a camera shutter. "You remember," she says quietly.

And suddenly I do. I remember everything about it. I remember that her hair was much shorter then, exposing her neck, and that she was wearing large sunglasses so that I couldn't see her eyes, and I remember her bare and shapely legs and the skirt she was wearing. And I remember that the damage to my truck was minimal but the damage to her Honda Accord was substantial, and I remember her scent wafting over to me on the breeze as she apologized profusely, and that I had been so taken with her that it took me two days to work up the courage to call her. I tell her all of this as she sits spellbound, as if hearing it all for the first time.

When I finish speaking she says to me, "I've always wondered something. How did you know I was single?"

"I didn't," I tell her, "but I didn't see a ring."

She reaches over the table and takes my hand again. "I'm glad you called," she says breathily, and for the first time since I woke up, I'm glad for something too.

[3.1]

Later, after some not-so-gentle prodding from my Moscato-filled wife, we go to bed together, and after some time, we collapse in a heap like marionettes without any strings, our skin searing and slippery from sex, our breath like steam, and she whispers my name as I finish. I'm holding myself up motionlessly on top of her for a moment, catching my breath, and she's looking so deeply into my eyes that I quickly disengage from her and roll over onto my back beside her, staring up at the ceiling, my mind completely blank, void of any thoughts or emotions, the physical feeling already beginning to fade away. The lamp on the bedside table is on, bathing her naked body in soft lighting, and the ceiling fan is running on the lowest setting, the slight breeze it produces cooling our respective sheens of sweat. She sighs a satisfactory sigh and pulls the rumpled bedsheet up over her legs to her hips and rolls toward me; her head feels warm and almost weightless resting upon my chest and her hair draped over and across my stomach smells like damp flowers and tickles my ribs when I breathe. I am absently twisting a delicate strand of it around my fingers and she is looking up at me with eyes like a deer—all big and moist and shiny—and she opens up her pretty little mouth to speak but no sound comes out, moves her soft lips but no words are formed, and no ideas are exchanged. She snuggles up closer to me.

I follow a single blade of the ceiling fan with my eyes, watching intently as an optical illusion of sorts causes the fan to appear to stand perfectly still as my eyes move. I instinctively know that I should say something loving and reassuring to her, but I don't—not because there is nothing for me to say, but because there is no real way for me to say it to her.

I can smell the Moscato on her breath as she breathes into my chest. A single fly buzzes overhead. A dog is barking ferociously somewhere off in the distance, or then again, maybe it isn't. My own dog lays sleeping, deep-breathing in its dog bed. The fly lands on my wife's shoulder to clean itself and lay eggs.

The whole time we lay there, until I drift off to sleep, I never brush it away.

[3.2]

There's a particular house on a particular street not unlike all the other houses set upon the same street where the traffic always goes by faster than the conservative posted speed limit of thirty-five miles per hour, and I'm twenty-two years old and I'm at a party at this particular house, standing in a freshly cut front yard talking to a pretty girl with dyed-red hair, long and straight with bangs down to her eyebrows, and she's slightly younger than me, with throwback hip-hugging bellbottom jeans and a yellow half-shirt which shows off her pierced belly-button, and she's got soft, smooth, lotion-smelling skin, and I'm pretending to listen to her as she speaks because I've got heady plans for her later in the evening, when the party winds down. And there are other people milling about the front yard as well, as well as many more inside the house, where the music is coming from, some of whom I know, many of whom I do not—some my own age and some slightly younger, and some significantly older, those late-twenty-somethings and even thirty-somethings that always insert themselves into the lives of the younger to feel more alive and in control—and everyone is conversing in small, tight-knit groups as the cars keep speeding by, and I'm holding a warm bottle of beer in my hand, the condensation wetting my palm, and I'm sharing a marijuana joint with the red-haired girl, who isn't wearing sunglasses and has to squint her eyes against then glare of the sun as she rambles on and on about nothing of any real significance or consequence. And someone has brought their dog along with them—or then again maybe it's just the local neighborhood stray—and I can't make out the breed, a mutt of some kind, but it's big and playful and seemingly happy to be in such fine company, panting hard in the heat of the day, a big, broad smile splitting its face as it prances about the yard, and the people all stand there rooted like trees, talking and smoking and drinking, and subconsciously releasing pheromones aimed at the opposite sex. And the minutes drag by, weighed-down heavy and slowed by the humid Florida heat, and at one point, a singularity in time, I'm about to reply to something the red-haired girl has just said to me when I hear the unmistakable sound of tires screeching—of heavy rubber biting down hard on hot asphalt—and I look away from the pretty red-haired girl just in time to see the dog get hit by a truck. It careens forward, twisting and tumbling violently through the air and skipping across the road before coming to an abrupt stop, and the sound that escapes from its lungs is the sound of a horror-movie shriek being expelled from a large red balloon as it is popped suddenly. The red-haired girl gasps, chokes on marijuana smoke, and a collective intake of breath can be heard arising from the throng of people gathered in the front yard; a disheartening beat of silence ensues, broken up by the sound of a solitary airplane moving past high overhead, filled with people who have no idea of the terrible thing that is happening on the ground thousands of feet below them. I instantly find myself moving toward the heap of dog lying motionless in the street, drawn to it instinctively, in much the same way a firefighter is drawn to the flames whilst everyone else is panicking and running the opposite way. Heat rises up from the asphalt in visible waves. The truck that hit the dog has stopped in the middle of the road, the traffic already beginning to build up behind it, and the dog is a pile of matted, slightly malodorous fur, unmoving, perhaps dead, perhaps momentarily stunned, completely still as I approach it. I can hear the red-haired girl asking me in a strained voice if its dead but just as her words enter my ears I can see the dog's leg twitching slightly as I get closer; the closer I get, the more animated the animal becomes: it's still alive. It tries to lift its head but it's unable to do so—its skull just keeps falling back down onto the street with a hollow thud, and there's blood pooling in the road already—I can imagine it bubbling and steaming as it cooks upon the searing blacktop. Upon reaching the dog, I first notice the organs and intestines spilling out of its abdomen—and the dog, the shock beginning to wear off now, becoming fully aware of what is happening to it, it's licking at its stomach between piercing yelps of complete and utter anguish. My eyes fall upon a spleen shining slick and wet upon the street—or then again, maybe it's a kidney. Behind me, clinging to my back, the red-haired girl is crying audibly; other more disjointed sobs can be heard from the other girls in the yard as well, and one of the older guys whom I do not know has followed me out to the road and when he sees the dog and the state it's in he says, simply, "Dude," and turns away. The dog is growing hysterical now, making noises that can neither be described nor replicated, and it doesn't seem to know what to do so it keeps trying to stand up but its legs aren't working properly—probably due to spinal injury—and so it keeps falling back down into the growing pool of blood with a sickening splat. A man exits the truck that hit the dog slowly, at half-speed, his radio turned up loud enough for me to hear from where I'm standing next to the dog, and the man's face is a pallid white color but I can't see the look in his eyes because, unlike the red-haired girl, the man is wearing sunglasses which hide his eyes from view. "I didn't see it," he keeps saying over and over, a self-comforting mantra, to anyone who will listen to him, and I'm idly wondering who actually owns this dog as we all stand there watching it suffer—maybe no one does. Just maybe, this poor and simple creature will be forced to die in terrifying agony with no one it knows and loves by its side to comfort it in its last moments. So it goes. Suddenly, a slight breeze activates itself into existence and glides by; I can smell the red-haired girl standing directly beside me now, no longer hiding behind me, putting on a brave face. She puts a hand over her mouth when she sees the dog up close, vomits when it makes eye contact with her. And floating toward us on the breeze are strains of music and melody coming from the truck's speakers, something ominous and dark and haunting, the words and you run and you run to catch up with the sun but it's sinking, racing around to come up behind you again, the sun is the same in a relative way but you're older, shorter of breath and one day closer to death *audible above all the terrible sounds which surround me, and the man, after a long moment of standing there and taking in the scene with slumped shoulders, suddenly straightens himself and walks purposefully back to his truck; he returns momentarily, holding a pistol. The sight of the pistol brings about a very real and very immediate and very visceral reaction from those people spectating safely from the front yard—some protest vehemently, some spout encouraging words, some remain deathly silent but for their collective gasps. "Oh my God," breathes the red-haired girl next to me, clutching my upper arm, "please don't let him shoot it." The man looks at me, as if awaiting permission; I look upon the tableaux in the road and then at the red-haired girl, and I peer deep into her oceanic eyes and I tell her that, in any situation, the best thing a person can do is the right thing. The second-best thing a person can do is the wrong thing. But the absolute worst thing a person can do is nothing. She takes this in, blinking away tears from her eyes, and, after a long moment of silent introspection, seeking to understand, she finally nods her head at me ever-so-slightly, and she covers her ears with her hands, to muffle the sound of the gunshot, but her eyes remain wide open and fixed upon the man holding the pistol. The man in turn nods at me, having heard what he needed to hear in order to do what needs to be done, and he walks up to the dog, holding the pistol outstretched in front of him, taking careful aim, and he says to me, "Is this your dog?" and when I shake my head no he immediately and without hesitation shoots the creature in the head, two shots in quick succession, fragments of blood and bone and brain matter splattering down onto the pavement at the same faster-than-sound speed as the slugs, and the animal drops down instantly, forever silent, forever still. The reverberations from the gun blasts seem to circle the earth, immediately quieting the birds in the trees above us, and for one brief and powerful moment, all is silent but for the man with the pistol saying, "I always hoped I'd never have to use this thing," and the voice from the truck's speakers is singing* the time is gone, the song is over, thought I'd something more to say. *Jump to the sound of sirens screaming in the distance. The people at the party immediately begin to disperse, the red-haired girl among them (so it goes) and soon, it's just the man holding the pistol and me holding my warm beer standing there looking at the dog lying dead in the street. The birds have resumed their singing once again and cars drive slowly around us—life going on—and for sure, in all other parts of the universe, it never really stopped at all. The sun goes behind a cloud; the man with the pistol takes off his sunglasses. His eyes are black as a moonless night, and he's crying . . . .*

I wake up and open my eyes to the suffocating darkness that engulfs me and I can feel my heart beating fast and strong in my chest and I can hear the blood rushing hot in my ears and I pull off the covers, allowing the nightmare-sweat to evaporate from my skin, and I have to wonder to myself, was it really just a dream, or was it a memory?

[4.1]

My wife is standing in front of the mirror in her mismatched-colors bra and panties, curling her long brunette hair into tresses, and I'm drying off from my shower, the edges of the mirror she's peering into blurred by steam, the smell of her lotion permeating the bathroom, and she's laid out a little blue dress on the bed. The dog looks at me lazily; we played "tug" before I got in the shower at the urging of my wife and now he seems to be all worn out.

"What time is it?" my wife wants to know, looking with concentration at her own reflection in the mirror and not at mine as she speaks.

"I don't know, maybe five," I tell her as I pull on a pair of boxer shorts.

"They'll probably be here soon," she says, in reference to Mike and Laura, and then, "we're having steaks tonight. Mike insisted on grilling." A puff of steam coils upward from her curling iron as she adds another tress. I walk up beside her and look at my own reflection. She clipped my hair before I showered; it looks better now, shorter and tighter, but I only let her trim my beard, despite her strong objections. I comb it out before wandering into the closet and picking out a shirt.

"Can you let Rambo out, hon?" she asks me as she begins putting on mascara. The dog looks up at the sound of its name and the word "out."

"Okay," I say, snapping my fingers at the dog, who immediately jumps to his feet and follows me to the back sliding-glass door. I let him out into the backyard, which is framed nicely by a seven-foot privacy fence. I'm anxious that my wife won't be ready in time before our guests arrive and I'll be forced to entertain them by myself, but it doesn't take long for her to skillfully apply her makeup and pull on that little blue dress; by the time I'm letting the dog back inside the house, she's meeting me in the kitchen.

"Well—how do I look?" she wants to know. She spins around playfully.

"Pretty," I say.

She smiles at me. "Oh my husband," she says spiritedly, coming toward me, "you sure have a way with words. You know just what to say to a girl." She kisses me. "I look forward to your next syllable with great eagerness." She winks.

I move to wrap my arms around her but she deftly slides away from me, eluding my grasp. "Don't mess up my hair," she warns. And then, right on cue, the doorbell rings.

The dog barks once, sits down patiently by the front door. My wife glides over to the door and opens it with a flourish to reveal a man and woman standing there on our front porch holding grocery bags. He's slightly shorter than me but more muscular, clean shaven, about the same age as me, with a professional-looking haircut; she's significantly shorter than my wife, pretty, probably a few years younger. They look at me; I look at them. A beat of silence ensues.

And then: "Hey!" my wife and Laura both exclaim in unison as they hug one another. Mike steps around them and into the house before setting down the grocery bags and extending his hand to me. I shake his hand, making direct eye-contact with him; he does the same, squeezes slightly harder than I do, his grip dry and warm and friendly.

Laura wants a hug. She steps up close and wraps her arms around me, squeezes tightly before pulling away and holding me at arm's length, studying my face. "Look at this beard!" she chirps, her hand snaking out toward my face and her fingers grabbing my chin hair. "You look so different."

"And distinguished," Mike adds good-naturedly with a wink toward my wife. "There's definitely some grey showing through in there, bud," he points out. I touch my jaw pensively.

"Oh, he looks just as handsome," Laura says with a dismissive wave of her hand.

"Well, don't get used to it," my wife says playfully, after giving Mike a hug hello. "It's coming off eventually."

I'm looking at Laura smiling grandly at me and then I look at Mike, who's looking at me as well, and I feel somewhat awkward, so much so that I find myself blurting out, "I'm sorry I don't remember you."

Laura responds immediately. "It's okay, you will soon enough." She pauses, continues. "It's just so good to see you home and well. We were so worried about you. Weren't we, babe?"

She looks over at Mike, who is looking at his phone. "Oh, yeah, you gave us quite a scare, bud," he agrees without looking up at me. Momentarily, he puts his phone back in his front khaki pocket and picks up the bags of groceries he'd been carrying and says to me, "Come on, I'm thirsty. Let's get a drink."

I pick up the grocery bags that Laura had been carrying and follow behind him; the dog follows as well.

[4.2]

Mike and I are in the garage talking and drinking beer and it's nice and cool because I have an air conditioner running and Mike is talking and I'm just listening as he guides the conversation along mostly superficial lines, telling me what I've missed in the world of sports (the heavyweight boxing championship has changed hands, the NFL preseason is about to begin, the Florida baseball teams are doing awful) and what I've missed as far as current events are concerned (the president continues to be a jackass, there's been not one but two mass shootings, the Florida wildfires continue). The dog is lying on a twin mattress on the floor in a corner of the garage, which is really more of a workshop than an actual garage, with woodworking equipment that I'm not quite sure how to properly operate, and a flat-screen TV mounted on the wall above a workbench cluttered with tools, some of which I *do* remember how to use. There's a pile of sawdust in one corner of the garage and an unfinished wooden chair nearby—apparently, I'm pretty good with my hands. There's also a refrigerator near the door stocked with Guinness and Budweiser, from which Mike and I are drinking. All this time I'm looking around the garage and taking it all in, thankfully, Mike is doing most of the talking.

During our somewhat one-sided conversation I learn that he is a detective with the Florida Department of Law Enforcement, homicide division, that he and Laura (who works in real estate) have been married for almost four years (both are divorcees) and that they have no children either. As I'm finishing up my beer, Mike is talking about a case that his younger brother, who also works for the Florida Department of Law Enforcement, vice division, just closed involving sex workers and wealthy out-of-state businessmen in the Orlando resort area.

"Some of these girls were only fifteen, sixteen years old," he's saying incredulously as he opens another beer. "The D.A., of course, she's going to paint these girls out to be victims, because they're under eighteen and all that, and of course the men we arrested with them will be charged with sex-crimes against minors and be forced to register as sex-offenders, but in all reality, these girls knew exactly what they were doing, and they were doing it willingly. They were making money hand over fist. And they were cold as ice when we questioned them about it." We're both quiet for a moment and after that moment passes he says to me, "So what's it like? Not remembering, I mean. I guess it's all you know right now, huh?"

I shrug. "It's strange," I say, searching my mind for the right words to describe how I feel, an exercise I find to be mired in futility. I'm about to open my mouth to add something but in that moment the garage door opens and my wife's head appears.

"Hello, boys," she singsongs, "are we finished hiding out in the mancave?" She smiles slyly. "What are we talking about, anyway?"

I answer back with, "Mike was telling me about this case where these—"

"Oh, NO!" she interrupts, coming into the garage and pointing a finger at Mike, "no, no, no. Save the crime talk for me, mister. You know how much I like hearing about your cases." She's almost pouting.

"Don't worry," Mike says, holding up his hands, "I've got a few for you. Pleasant dinner conversation for sure. *Now*—how are the sides coming along in there? I'm ready to throw those steaks on the grill. How about you, bud? You hungry?"

I nod. My wife announces that everything is ready, smiles at me and turns around to walk back through the door and into the house. I catch Mike eyeing her closely as she does so.

The look in his eyes is that of a cheetah staring down a gazelle.

[4.3]

The four of us are seated around the dining room table eating our steaks and potatoes and asparagus and salad and drinking our beers (the guys) and our wine (the girls) and Mike is talking about the big case he's working on that my wife has seen stories about on the evening news.

"We've got six missing girls from four different college towns along the I-4 corridor," he's saying as we all listen raptly. "In each case, all that's been left behind is their shoes. That's the only way we know they're all connected."

"Their *shoes*?" my wife and I both ask incredulously.

"Yup," Mike says, "just the shoes. It's some kind of sick calling card, I guess. Whoever is taking these girls must like them barefooted. We're keeping that out of the press, by the way, to weed out the false confessions. We're also looking into that whole foot fetish thing— websites, chatrooms, whatever—the tech guys are all over it. We need any and all leads on this one."

We all think about this silently. "Talk about a needle in a haystack," my wife says finally. "Lots of guys like feet." She winks at me secretively. Mike nods affirmatively.

"You're right, there's a lot of weirdos out there. But we have to be proactive. These girls, they're not high-risk victims like drug addicts or runaways or prostitutes. They come from good homes. They were all young and pretty and smart—five out of the six were enrolled in college courses, and two of the girls' shoes were found right there in campus parking lots." He pauses, takes a bite of steak before continuing. "With the press, we use phrases like 'similar circumstances' and 'possibly connected' and 'persons of interest' but I think we're dealing with one guy who's abducted all these girls. God only knows what he's doing with them. I don't hold out much hope that they're still alive. But we haven't found any bodies so far. And no physical evidence whatsoever—except the shoes of course, but like I said before, we're keeping that out of the press. They've just up and vanished."

"Why would anyone give a false confession?" I find myself wondering aloud. Mike looks at me gravely.

"You'd be surprised, bud," he says, shaking his head. "You'd be very surprised."

"But how do you know, exactly?" my wife asks, completely enthralled, through a mouthful of food.

"Know what?" Mike wants to know.

"That it's just one guy?"

Mike gulps down the rest of his beer, gets up from the table to get another, shakes his empty bottle at me, signaling to me, silently asking if I'd like another. I nod my head yes. "Well, I don't know *for sure*," he says over his shoulder, "but, by all accounts, these were *good* girls—no way they'd go off alone somewhere with two or three strange men. And they didn't appear to be blitz attacks—at least not initially. No one heard any screams and there was no sign of a struggle where we found the shoes. It's just a feeling that I have—team killers are extremely rare; it's possible, but I think these girls were approached by just one guy, a single, non-threatening male—he's either young enough to fit in with the college crowd or he's an older authority figure. Maybe he's even got a fake badge or something." He sits back down at the table and his eyes narrow, that hard look you see from old-west sheriffs when they squint their eyes against the sun in western movies. "Ted Bundy used a fake cast to disarm his victims. He also used a fake badge. I can see this guy doing the same thing. In any case, he isn't out of place in these college towns. He looks like he belongs. Hell, he fits right in. He approaches them with some kind of ruse and then, at some point, as soon as they've let their guard down, he gets control over them. And then, off come the shoes." He goes quiet for a moment. "We'll get him," he finally says. "The FBI is coming in on Monday."

We're all quiet for a somber minute or so, taking it all in, fascinated by Mike's powers of deduction. I take the last few bites of my steak and wipe my mouth with a napkin before sitting back in my chair, sipping a fresh beer and looking over at my wife; I can see the wheels in her head spinning away—her intellectual interest clearly piqued. Laura, however, is in a lamenting mood.

"I just can't understand all the terrible things that people do to one another. I'll never get used to hearing about it, no matter how long he does it."

"You never really get used it, honey. You just learn to set it aside," Mike tells her.

"Well, some things I just can't get out of my mind," she continues. "Like the case you just had about the baby. I still wake up thinking about it."

"Oh my God, a *baby*?" my wife asks horrified, her eyes wide.

"Well, before you get too upset, the baby is fine," Mike says, his tone perfectly even. "There was a young woman in Jacksonville who was found eviscerated—turns out she'd been nine months pregnant at the time—and the baby was gone." He pauses to drink from his beer, creating dramatic effect. "Long story short, it turns out that another woman who had recently found out that she couldn't have children had been stalking the pregnant woman for days before finally forcing her into a car, driving her to a field, strangling her unconscious, and cutting out the baby using her car keys. She then took the baby for herself and left the other woman to bleed to death right there in a field of wildflowers. Needless to say, that was a tough one to swallow."

"How'd you catch her?" I ask.

Mike shrugs. "It was easy, actually. We used the press, told the public to be on the lookout for someone who wasn't pregnant before but now had a baby. Someone called us a week later—a member of the suspect's family, in fact. When we arrested her, she confessed immediately, like it was no big deal. The only time she showed any emotion at all was when we took the baby away from her."

"That's *terrible*," is all my wife can muster to say. I simply nod in agreement. Mike shrugs again. Laura sits there staring at her food and looking sick.

"Hey, I *told* you I'd have some riveting dinner conversation for you," Mike says to my wife, his tone completely different. He turns in his chair to face me. "So, bud, the preseason starts on Thursday night. We watching the game at your house or mine?"

I'm amazed how quickly he can go from morbid to benign.

It must take years of practice.

[5.1]

After bidding Mike and Laura goodnight some time later, my wife and I are lying in bed, talking and watching the eleven o'clock news, and sure enough, there's a news story about the missing girls that

Mike was talking about. Splashed across the screen are pictures of pretty, young, smiling faces taken from varying social media platforms, with their names scrawled across the bottom of the screen, wholesome American-girl names like Amber and Heather and Stephanie written in large-type graphics below screenshots of selfies lifted from Facebook and Instagram, and the newspersons reiterate that each girl vanished without a trace, and that the police have no suspects, and that the FBI will be joining forces with the FDLE and the local authorities in the hopes of breaking the case. "Can you imagine?" my wife breathes, shaking her head, eyes glued to the screen. "That Miller girl was taken only fifteen miles away from here at Seminole State College. He was so close by, just lurking and hunting our girls, and no one even knew it. It's just so unbelievable."

I agree with her, though I find my mind wandering, my fingers walking up and down my wife's hips and thigh, tickling her slightly; she giggles and pushes my hand away, snuggles up even closer. Because we've both been drinking, our body heat is radiating outward at a higher frequency than normal, and I throw off the comforter, leaving only the sheet to cover our nakedness as my hand wanders, exploring her skin, only to be batted away playfully by my wife.

"You know what I miss?" she asks me, her face nuzzled into my chest.

"What's that?" I ask her.

"Your stories. You used to tell me stories while we laid here in bed at night. I miss that."

I think about this for a minute, racking my brain, and yet, no story comes to mind. "I guess I've forgotten them all," I say, eyes on the TV as the sports anchor discusses the upcoming preseason football game between the Jacksonville Jaguars and the Detroit Lions, the very game that Mike and I made plans to watch this upcoming Thursday evening, lest he be tied up at work. And then, I get an idea. "Why don't you tell me one?" I ask my wife as soon as a commercial comes on.

She sits up some, rests her weight on an elbow, turns her head to look at me. "*You're* the one with all the stories," she retorts, though she seems open to the idea.

"Come on," I press, nestling down comfortably into the mattress, "tell me a story."

"Okay," she says, adjusting herself in the bed so that her head is resting upon my chest, "this is a story you've told me before, about Archimedes." She pauses for effect, continues. "Back in the days when Ancient Greece was a world power, it wasn't a unified country. It was a scattering of city states called *polises*, each with its own king, or kings, as was the case with the Spartans. Anyway, the kings were paid their tributes in gold, in the form of beautiful statuettes or be-jeweled crowns or other pieces of art sculpted in gold, the worth of each piece calculated by its weight; however, there was no way to know for certain if a piece was solid gold or merely gold-plated with-out having it melted-down, thus destroying it. So, the king of Syra-cuse employed a man named Archimedes with the task of discerning whether or not something was solid gold or simply gold-plated with-out having to melt it down. Archimedes thought about the problem day and night—he became obsessed with it and consumed by it, to the point where he stopped eating or bathing. Finally, his poor wife had had enough and forced Archimedes to take a bath. So, he filled a bathtub with water, and when he got in it, he noticed that the water rose—he had discovered displacement—and the answer to the prob-lem he had been obsessing over came to him instantly. Elated, he jumped out of the bath and ran naked through the streets of Syracuse screaming the word 'Eureka!' which in his Greek tongue meant 'I have found it!'"

"So," I say rubbing her back with my hand, "the moral of the story is, whenever you're faced with an insurmountable problem, take a step back, and the answers will come."

"No," she says, lifting her head to look at me, her face inches from mine, "the moral of the story is, always listen to your wife." She kisses me lightly on the lips. I smile.

The dog dep breathes in his dog bed. My wife falls asleep quickly; I listen to her deep breathing and time my own breaths with hers, so that we're inhaling and exhaling at exactly the same time. I reach over and turn off the lamp on the bedside table and I lie there with my eyes closed, concentrating on the symphony of our breath, until I softly drift to sleep.

[5.2]

During the night I find myself dreaming of dreadful things, of darkened corners and glowing red eyes, of supple young flesh sheened in sour panic-sweat and slowly being parted with a sharp knife, the blood seeping out so fast it's still blue, until the nitrogen and oxygen in the air hits it and turns it red, and of terrified eyes opened as wide as they are able, tears of pain streaming down flushed cheeks and dripping from quivering chins, and of screams—horrid, scathing screams which echo within the caverns of my mind, reverberating off the insides of my skull—and of endless digging, hole after hole, for what seems like an eternity in a dark space where time has all but stopped. These images replay themselves over and over in my mind's eye, no doubt influenced by the lurid subject matter that made up our dinner conversation, until I finally, after a night of deep-yet-restless sleep, I open my eyes to the morning sun spilling in the window, flecks of dust dancing in the sunbeam like confetti swirling around the room, the air still, the screams but a remnant deep in the middle of my ears.

My wife has already left for work—I never heard her stirring—
and it's just me and the dog in the house for the next eight hours or
so. I get out of bed and get dressed, splash some cold water on my
face, the uneasiness of the dreams slowly fading away from my consciousness, and I let the dog outside. Despite it only being nine-thirty
in the morning the sky is already hot and blue and endless, and full of
possibility and open opportunity and swarming with flying insects
which dart manically about. The occasional larger-than-life hole dots
the fragile, paper-thin ozone layer from the careless overspraying of
chlorofluorocarbons, and from giant plumes of methane gas and car-
bon monoxide emissions, causing the mass-meltings of glaciers and
polar ice caps—whole icebergs breaking apart, steadily raising sea lev-
els and eroding once-beautiful coastlines. And cancer cells rain down
within the suspect radiance of brilliantly-hued sunbeams which light
upon the sound of children laughing and playing, carefree youthful
levity hanging on the gentlest of summer breezes, and flies find rot-
ting meat and baby birds leave the nest and fly for the first time or
fall to their deaths, and all the while the sun continues to climb slowly
and steadily into the sky, waiting for no one or nothing. I let the dog
back inside.

There isn't much for me to do with myself so I decide to look
around the house, make myself familiar with where things are, maybe
glean some insight into who I really was, and, by extension, who I really am. The bookshelves catch my attention first. I look at all the
books all arranged in alphabetical order by the author's last name and
marvel at the idea that I have poured over them all so eagerly over
the years, hungrily ingesting the knowledge offered within the bind-
ings, carefully-yet-relentlessly turning their dog-eared pages until my
eyes grew weary and my mind was set aglow with provocative ideas
and new-perspective insights. Some of the books have existed far
longer than I myself have, and will continue to exist long after I am

gone from this world, and some are newer, wrapped in shiny dust jackets and full of updated information, a natural linear progression from some of the older books as science and thought have advanced steadily throughout the years. Some of the books are classics, written in flowery prose; some are more modern, minimalistic and novel. Some of the more interesting books speak to the nature of man, and a collective consciousness—an idea that all human beings are connected to one another through a supposed set of shared beliefs, ideals, and moral attitudes—a communal understanding of what is good and evil, of what is right and wrong—and of social obligation, of assumed responsibilities, a social contract taken on by each individual choosing to exist among other human beings within a closed society—and the importance of adhering to this unspoken covenant in order to further the best interests of said society. And still, other books speak to a polar opposite of the same reality—one of a differing opinion which states that nothing can be labeled as good or bad because nothing really matters at all—that there is no divine, no evil, no right or wrong—only meaningless, randomly meandering life until death—and, much like Ptolemy's geocentric universe as opposed to Copernicus' heliocentric model of the same universe, only the inevitable passage of time and the steady gathering of knowledge will ultimately prove which is correct.

After spending considerable time perusing the books I find myself in the garage, the workshop where I spend, according to my wife, the bulk of my spare time. There's a radio on the workbench; I turn it on, put the volume on low, to provide a background soundtrack to my sleuthing. I open drawers, my eyes falling upon tools of varying sorts, most of which look well-used yet well taken care of. I find a drawer with drawings in them, not exactly crude but not professional-looking either, and I assume they were made by me. There's drawings of chairs and tables with measurements and angles labeled precisely, and of a great three-tiered wooden deck that does not yet exist—it must be a future project—and one that appears to be a gazebo, also not yet built. As things stand now, I doubt I would be able to build such things, though there is the sliver of hope in my chest that allows me to believe it will be possible again one day. There are shelves above the workbench and along the exterior wall of the garage, upon most of which sit tools of various kinds, electrical saws and the like, and I pick up these items by their handles, sensing the heft of their weight in my hand, getting re-accustomed to their feel. Behind one such tool, on the highest shelf in the garage, sits an old cigar box, an old rag draped over it, obscuring it from view. Curious, I take it down from the shelf; it's very light, but it isn't quite empty; I can feel something shift inside of it.

Upon opening the box, I find a small stack of driver's licenses. The pictures on the licenses are all of pretty young girls, with All-American names like Amber and Heather and Stephanie, and they look oddly familiar to me but I can't place exactly why at first, but in time, in staring at them, shuffling through them over and over again, the garage around me slowly begins to fade away into the background, becoming more of a backdrop than an actual setting, feeling less and less like a familiar place and more and more like a cell or a grave of some kind, and the air I'm breathing suddenly goes thin and stale, tasting acrid and dry, and I feel more isolated and alone in this moment of space and time than I ever have in my whole life as the realization eventually comes to me that I have seen these girls, their names and their pictures, before, in stories about missing girls on the evening news, and I have heard their agonized screams in my sleep, and I have dug their holes in my dreams.

The Thirteenth Step

1997

"*G*od, *grant me the serenity to accept the things I cannot change, the courage to change the things I can, and the wisdom to know the difference.*"

Twelve other people aside from myself, of differing ages, genders, backgrounds and social statuses are all seated around one another in a tight circle, in suspended orbit around the empty center of the room in small, uncomfortable metal chairs, and they're all reciting these words in rote unison during a Narcotics Anonymous meeting, which is being held in the First Methodist Church in Cherryville, two towns over from where I live in Park City, and I'm saying these words right along with everyone else but they hold no real meaning for me, because I do not principally believe in a higher power of any kind, nor am I a recovering addict. Tonight, this particular gathering of losers, degenerates, misfits and unfortunates is being led by a man known to us as Hester—middle-aged, with a greasy, graying ponytail and goatee, and thick glasses which distort his eyes and make them appear far larger than they actually are—a former methamphetamine addict and self-described born-again Christian who has, by his own count, been clean and sober now for close to four years, all praise be to his own personal Lord and Savior Jesus Christ, through whom all things are possible, Amen. And I'm sitting here present in body and appearance in this little circle of trust and I'm hearing these people and their sob stories but I'm really only half-listening because my mind is elsewhere, though I do appear to be fully engaged when someone points out that we're all powerless over our addictions, because I'm not here in this church tonight for whatever it is these people are here for and hope to gain for themselves by being here, I'm really only here for the girl.

There's an older woman here named Janice who was probably relatively pretty before all the drugs and the children and all the stresses of being alive in this particular place and time, and she's tearfully regaling the group with a story about how her intravenous heroin addiction has ruined not only her finances and her marriage but also her relationship with her now-estranged children as well, and as she speaks I'm looking around the circle at the faces of the people listening intently to her testimonial and I can see the sympathy and empathy etched into their faces but no matter how hard I try, no matter how much I wish it to be so, I cannot seem to will myself into actually *feeling* it, though I do mimic their expressions of concern well. And, while I cannot physically share in their empathetic response to Eric's sympathy-inducing stimuli when he's telling the group about how his addiction to crack-cocaine caused him to prostitute himself to older men with money, despite the fact that he isn't gay, I do feel somewhat sorry for them all in my own way, in that they're not even really alive anymore, in that they have simply traded one life-altering addiction for another—sobriety for drugs—and in that they seem to expend even more energy and fervor into staying clean and sober than they ever did in their zest for getting high.

And, as the Janices and Erics of the group speak aloud about hard times and indiscretions and tears stream down somber faces, the girl just sits there silently, sullen and expressionless, completely unmoved. She's positioned at my eleven-o'-clock, which affords me a very good view of her from where I'm sitting (this is by no accident, of course)— she has long black hair and she's wearing tight jeans and a long jacket, and red lipstick, and though I do not particularly care much for lipstick, she does have a nice body and her face isn't all beat-up-looking like some of the other girls who attend these meetings. And she's periodically gnawing at her fingernails and relentlessly bouncing her crossed leg up and down as she sits there in her uncomfortable little chair listening to a seemingly endless stream of sad-sack stories, a telltale sign of opioid withdrawal, and she doesn't appear to be here with anyone else, so she has become the target—the one I'm zeroing in on—my injured little gazelle.

And as the meeting drags on and on and these hopeless people drone on and on about their respective rock bottoms and subsequent resurfacings, and about how they're all just taking it one day at a time, the girl and I make eye contact a few times, and I smile at her a very well-practiced and very benign-looking smile; she responds back with a kind of forced, tight-lipped grimace—all she can really muster in her dope-sickness—and she fidgets with her necklace and bounces that legs up and down, periodically flipping her hair from one side of her head to the other and back again, all futile attempts to speed up time and fast-forward to the end of the meeting.

Fast-forward to the end of the meeting. Hester finally dismisses the group with the program's catchphrase "it works if you work it" and people either linger behind to help detail the next meeting or get another cup of free coffee and conversate amongst themselves or they meander outside into the cool January air for a much-needed cigarette—smoking being one of the more prevalent characteristics of N.A.ers—and when the girl, who did not speak at all during the entire course of the meeting, goes directly outside and lights up a cigarette, I do the same, although I don't normally smoke. She's isolated herself away from a small group of fellow smokers; I position myself a non-threatening eight paces away from her, my body turned slightly toward her but my eyes looking upward into the clear night sky, focusing upon the planet Venus, which, on a moonless night such as tonight, is the brightest thing in the sky. Having no one else in our immediate vicinity is a good thing, because she has no one to talk to, and there is no one to keep her attention off me as I stand there. I can feel her looking at me but I keep my eyes trained on the heavens above us as I smoke my cigarette, intentionally ignoring her, waiting for her to take the first steps toward initiating interaction, as this is a key factor in disarming her—to mute the warning bells in her head, to make them moot points. I wait a beat, take another drag from my cigarette—a menthol, which tastes even worse than a full-flavor cigarette and burns my throat even worse as I inhale it, but which I have learned that drug addicts seem to prefer for some reason, so I always carry a pack of them with me to meetings—and I finally avert my eyes from the sky and glance over at her when I'm sure she's looking at me; she immediately looks away, shyly looking up and looking somewhat down, a kind of reticent sadness carved softly into her features, and she says quickly, hurriedly, "That star is really bright."

I follow her gaze up toward Venus. I look at it for a moment, take a drag, exhale audibly as I'm speaking to her. "I think that's a planet," I say, not wanting to intimidate her by appearing too knowledgeable about anything.

There's a tick of silence as she looks harder, squinting her eyes at it, a clear sign that she requires corrective lenses but isn't wearing them. "How can you tell?" she wants to know.

I shrug apathetically. "I don't know," I lie, "it just looks too bright to be a star, I guess. I could be wrong, though."

She continues to look upward, her gray eyes darting back and forth across the sky, comparing the brightness of Venus to the brightness of the stars in the same vicinity. "No, you're probably right," she sighs. "I wonder which planet it is?"

I don't answer. She trains her eyes on me as I'm looking her over; she looks me over in turn, not unimpressed by what she sees. She takes a drag from her cigarette and breathes a plume of smoke, scratches an eyebrow, shifts her weight from one foot to the other; I subtly mirror her movements to draw her in, casually move a step closer, but no more. I introduce myself, giving a fake name of course. "I'm Ursula," she says rather flatly, the inflection of her voice not really matching her more welcoming body language, which temporarily confuses me, until I factor in the dope-sickness I know she's feeling, and then it makes more sense.

Standing this much closer to her, I can see the blackness of her eyes, the want and the need spreading outward from her pupils in the form of dilation.

"Ursula like the actress?" I ask her, though I know of no actress named Ursula.

She sighs again. "No, Ursula like the villain from *The Little Mermaid*. You're thinking of Uma Thurman," she says somewhat sadly, looking down at her feet.

"Ah," I say, allowing a short silence to pass between us before speaking again. "I'm sorry."

"It happens," she says.

A rather longish silence this time, and then I say, "So, you waiting on a ride?"

"I need to make a phone call first," she says, motioning toward the pay phone bank at the gas station across the street, caddy-corner really. "I told my dad I'd call him when the meeting was over."

"Ah," I say again, "so you live at home?"

"For now," she says rather quickly, as what I can only assume is embarrassment spreads a reddish color across her pallid face. "I had to move back in after I got arrested." She pauses suddenly, looks at me closely, searching my face for a reaction, a judgment of some kind; there is none. She continues. "I hate it there. They treat me like a kid—like a prisoner—like I'm some kind of criminal. I swear, it's no different than jail."

I tell her I sure know all about overbearing parents. "What'd you get arrested for?" I ask, and then say, mock-apologetic, "I mean—I'm sorry, it's none of my business."

"No, it's okay," she assures me, takes two full steps closer to me. "I got caught with a gram of H." She shrugs. "It's not like I'm an addict like these people are," she says quietly, motioning toward the small cluster of people talking and smoking just outside the church doors. "I mean, I don't shoot up or anything—I just snort it." She pauses again, takes another drag of her cigarette which is already half gone. "Anyway, I got pulled over while smoking a joint and even though I tossed it, the cops smelled it and searched me and found the baggie in my bra. They actually called in a female cop just so they could search me, you believe that? Anyway, I spent a few days in jail before they released me into my parents' custody and put me into the program." She gestures toward the church. "And here we are."

"So you're court-ordered, huh?" I ask. She nods her head.

I'm guessing she gets drug-tested once a week. I'm guessing that they probably drug-tested her on Monday or Tuesday, right after the weekend. I'm guessing that she's perfect for me, perfect for tonight. I decide to chum the waters.

"Yeah, I hear you," I say, taking one last drag from my cigarette— I've smoked about all I can—before flicking it away into the night. "I got caught with some Vicodin," I lie again, "so now I'm court-ordered to come to these things twice a week. But I only get drug-tested once a week, so, you know . . . ." I let the sentence fragment hang there in the air for her to grab ahold of.

She continues to smoke her cigarette down to the filter. "Know what?" she finally wonders aloud. I take a quick look around, as if I'm making sure that no one is listening, and I lean in closer to her; she leans in closer as well—I'm now close enough to smell her unwashed hair. I lower my voice.

"Well, I don't know about heroin," I lie yet again, "but Vicodin only stays in your system for like, three days, tops. So, I can still take a few of them throughout the week, here and there, to keep from getting sick."

She's quiet for a moment, thinking about this, mulling it over. A car passes through the church parking lot, illuminating her face angel-like, making it seem as though a lightbulb is going off cartoon-style above her head. "I just took a drug test yesterday," she finally says.

"Me too," I say with a wink. "That's why tonight, as soon as I get home . . . ." I shrug, trailing off, allowing her to fill the empty space in the conversation with her own imagination.

She looks around, making sure that no one is listening, leans in even closer than before. "Do you have anything?" she whispers quietly, hopefully, her pupils big as dimes, staring right into me like two little abysses, pulling me in like black holes.

I shrug again. "Maybe," I say casually, purposely looking away from her, watching the people in the church parking lot pile into their respective vehicles and leave to return to their sad, dysfunctional lives. "It depends." I look back at her.

She scrunches up her face. "On what?" she asks somewhat innocently, somewhat defiantly.

I allow her question to linger on the slightest of breezes along with the desperation I know she is feeling before answering with a simple, "On you." Pause. "What's it worth to you?"

I look her over again. Gone is the friendliness from my face—a kind of cold matter-of-factness has now taken its place. She looks back at me for a long moment before saying quietly, sullenly, "I don't have any money." I stare at her. She looks away, pulls another Newport from out of her pack and lights it, inhaling the smoke and breathing it out at a much quicker pace than the pace she employed to smoke the first one. The seconds tick by; my heart beats just as slow, maybe even a bit slower, than an atomic clock. Hers, I'm quite sure, is beating much faster.

By not saying anything at all during this silence she has taken the bait—now it's time to simply set the hook and reel her in.

"You know, it's too bad you have to go home," I say casually, allowing her to see me looking her over. "You're a pretty girl—we could've had some fun." I let the implication sink in, so that there can be no mistake, so that she's fully aware of the price of those pills she so badly wants and needs.

To my pleasant surprise, she's not so young and naïve as she seems. She gets right to it, bridging the gap. "We could maybe do some oral in your car," she says very, very quietly.

"I don't have them with me," I say, trying to sound nonchalant, concealing my excitement with monotone. "Besides, oral wouldn't be enough for me. I would want more." I'm whispering this to her so that no one else can possibly hear me.

She thinks about this for a few moments, hems and haws silently, but not near as long as some of the others have in the past. This is usually the moment where they make a scene and/or storm away from me; Ursula, however, is different. She takes a drag from her cigarette, not really looking at me, but not really turning away from me either. "I would need a ride home after," she says barely audibly after a full minute has passed.

And just like that, negotiations have begun.

I answer immediately. "You'd need a shower first," I tell her.

She looks at me suspiciously, squinting her eyes to get a better look at me. "How do I know you're not some psycho killer or something like that?" she finally asks me.

I smile grandly at her, agreeably amused. "Well, Ursula," I say, pulling out my own pack of Marlboro menthols and lighting another one, in order to create some camaraderie between us, "I guess you don't. But even if I were, people have seen us talking together, and they'd see us leave together. If you turned up dead or missing, or even hurt in any way, I'd be the number-one suspect, wouldn't I?"

She looks at me somewhat strangely, as if to say *ohhh-kaaayyy*, but in mulling it over, seemingly pacified by my immediate and logical response, she finally gets around to asking me the all-important question of, "How many can I have?"

"Well," I say, "that depends."

She looks exasperated. "On what?"

"On what you let me do," I say matter-of-factly. I allow these words to sink in.

She looks directly at me again, very serious. "No rough stuff," she warns me, unapologetically.

I pretend to think about this, long enough so that she begins to feel nervous about what I have in mind for her—I can see it in her eyes—and though I want her to be uncomfortable, I don't want to scare her away, either, so I pretend to relent and allow her to feel as though she's won a concession, to make her feel as if she's in control of the situation.

Besides, I can always renegotiate later.

"Okay," I say, my tone pleasant, placid, almost whimsical, "how does five sound?"

It works like a charm. "Ten," she immediately retorts, with confidence. "Up front."

"You really think you're worth ten?" I smirk at her, fully enjoying the verbal jousting.

"It's either that, or you'll be using your hand tonight instead," she says coolly, exhaling smoke in my face.

Again, I pretend to think about it. "Eight," I finally say to her, evenly and sternly, with authority. "Four up front and four afterward. I don't have ten to give," I lie.

She sighs, looks away from me, watches cars drive past the church for what feels like a long time before finally relenting. "What are you driving?" she asks morosely, sighing audibly.

And just like that, negotiations are complete.

This almost never works for me. My success rate in coming to meetings and even just finding a viable candidate to *attempt* to take home with me is only around five percent or so, I'd say; my success rate in actually getting them to come home with me for sex is a much more dismal decimal-point or so percentage, so I'm literally vibrating with excitement as I lead her to my car and open the passenger-side door for her to get in.

Most times, I have to go home frustrated.

I'm not worried about people seeing her leave with me because I don't intend to do anything bad to her.

In the car she's flipping through my CD book looking for something to listen to and fidgeting with her necklace uncomfortably and I'm stealing glances at her as we drive down the road, and Cracker's "Low" is playing on the radio, WJRK, my favorite station, and I place my hand upon her upper thigh and squeeze as the chorus is being sung and she instantly tenses up her thigh muscle but she doesn't pull away or push my hand away or anything so I leave my hand there, feeling her warmth, squeezing her leg at random intervals, whenever I see fit. At one point she pulls a cigarette from out of her pack but before she can light it, I say, "Not in the car," and she puts it back into her pack, places the pack back into her purse, out of sight and out of mind.

And time passes; years go by; empires rise and fall to a soundtrack of alternative rock coming out of the speakers. Finally, still casually flipping through the CD book, she says, without looking at me, "You've done this before, haven't you?"

Taken aback, I feign ignorance.

She's not so young and naïve as she looks.

"What's that?" I ask innocently.

"This," she says almost insolently. "Take girls home in exchange for drugs."

I'm quiet for a moment, staring straight out the windshield at the road in front of me. I squeeze her thigh hard—she tenses again. I'm thoroughly enjoying this. "Does it really matter?" I eventually ask her.

"I guess not," she says coldly. "I just hope you have a condom."

"Don't worry," I say, turning up the radio to drown out her voice, "I do."

Eight minutes-worth of silence later she still hasn't decided upon a CD to play but it doesn't really matter anymore because I'm pulling into my driveway, and I turn off the headlights and the ignition and I exit the car without a word; she follows me closely to my front door, on my heels like a little puppy. Once inside the house I instruct her to sit on the living room couch and I offer her a beer, which she gladly accepts, and I retrieve two from the refrigerator, one for her and one for me, before wordlessly disappearing into my bedroom to count out her pills from the large bottle of Vicodin I have that I took from a girl's purse. I return to the living room with eight little white pills and place four of them into the palm of her clammy hand, watching intently as she swallows them one by one with sips of beer; the other four I place on the kitchen counter, in full view, so that she can see what she's working toward.

"Aren't you going to take any?" she asks me after she's swallowed the last one.

"I already did," I lie. I don't really think she believes me.

Not that I really care.

Earlier this morning, a Delta II rocket exploded mere seconds into its launch at Cape Canaveral; it was carrying something called a global positioning system (GPS) satellite that was worth about $45 million. Following the explosion, more than two-hundred-and-fifty tons of flaming rocket fuel and debris rained back down upon the earth like the wrath of God at Sodom and Gomorrah in front of a live television audience. Amazingly, no one was injured. I took this all as a sign.

"You have a very clean house," Ursula observes quietly.

"Thank you for noticing," I say, staring at her. She looks demurely away, takes another sip of beer. I'm ready to pounce. "Now—" I say to her, in my best getting-down-to-business voice, "would you like to sit here and make small talk until your pills kick in, or would you like to take your shower now?"

She takes in a deep breath, sharply. "Shower, I guess," she says barely audibly, looking down at her lap.

"Okay," I say, rubbing my hands together briskly, as I'm aching to see her naked, aching to actually *feel* her after all the foreplay, "follow me." She sucks down the rest of her beer and hands me the empty bottle, wiping her mouth with the back of her hand as she swallows, before rising up from the couch and following me through the house, past the living room with everything perfectly in its place, down the hallway and into the bedroom, where I usher her into the bathroom and take a fresh towel from the bathroom closet and place it upon the counter; I also take a brand-new disposable razor from under the sink and place it on top of the towel. She eyes the razor inquisitively. "I want you to shave as well," I tell her.

She looks at me kind of funny. "My legs?" she wants to know.

I glance down at her crotch area. "Everything," I tell her flatly. She picks up the razor, looks at the twin blades, looks back at me, blushes. Her eyes are pleading with me, but she doesn't say anything. "Go ahead," I whisper hoarsely, "get undressed."

She hesitates for the briefest of moments, and then, as I'm silently watching her, every inch of her, making her as uncomfortable as I can without scaring her, she shyly complies.

She's covering her breasts with her hands as she steps into the shower and I pull the shower curtain aside so that I can see her get wet and after she finally uncovers them I tell her, "You're very pretty," and I close the shower curtain and leave the bathroom, though I leave the door open. She showers for a very long time— they always do—and I drink the rest of my beer until I finally hear the water turn off, at which time I get undressed myself, so that, when she comes out of the bathroom, she can instantly see the state of excitement that I'm in.

And everything goes according to plan, and, even though she cries a little, which I like, and even though she pretty much lets me do everything I want to her, within reason, it still isn't nearly as exciting as I had anticipated, or satisfying enough to be worth all the time and effort I put into getting her here, and I'm left wholly unfulfilled once again. And it's that moment afterward, while she's getting re-dressed, her back to me, red-faced and trying to hide her nakedness from me as best she can, that I suddenly realize I enjoy the hunt a whole lot more than I do the meal itself.

MORS INDECEPTA

Quite often, it is very strange how things work themselves out. Some might even venture as far as to say that it is *funny* how things work out, but most times, there is nothing funny at all about the things that happen to us. Life is pain, as they say; to live is to suffer, and all that. This is the hard, true way of the Universe, and we are all astonishingly powerless to control it. But it is, all the same, quite often very strange how things tend to work themselves out.

I believe in Providence. I am of the belief that the Universe unfolds itself exactly as it should. Not that this belief makes things any easier to digest, mind you. It does not. And, to be sure, it is not that I do not attempt to alter the Universe's plans and course of action when they do not fit my own. There is, though, however small, a kind of cold comfort in knowing that, whatever terrible thing has just happened, you have tried your best, and there was nothing more you could have done differently to have stopped it from happening as it did. There was simply nothing you could have done to prevent it. It happened, and it would have happened eventually regardless of the steps you have taken along your path.

I truly believe this to be true, despite the pain it yet causes me from time to time.

I had a son. His mother raised him, in every sense of the word, but I watched him grow, and I surely loved him as I was able, in my own distant way. I afforded him guidance when I felt it appropriate to do so, exacted corporal punishment when his mother saw fit, and provided for him food, and shelter, and amenities, and even some frivolous comforts and possessions. As it was, he wanted for little and lacked for absolutely nothing; his mother and I saw to this, and he grew up happy and well, and secure.

He was a good boy; he gave us minimal troubles, as even the best behaved of children are wont to do from time to time, and through the years he grew to be an even better young man. His mother and I were proud of him, and we wanted only the best possible life for him, so we told him in no uncertain terms on many different occasions, *You are going to college*. In this, there was no room for argument—we had the money for his higher education, and he had the grades, as well as the scholarship offers, and, most importantly, he possessed the will and the drive to be successful, and so I took it as Total Providence when the acceptance letters began to arrive in the mail.

In my eyes, the stars were aligning, and everything was unfolding exactly as it should.

But then came the trouble, that curveball that the Universe tends to throw you when you're looking for a fastball. Our dear son had chosen a college out of state—to sever the cord from himself to his mother and I, so to speak, and as a man, I fully understood this course of action; his mother, my wife, however, simply could not accept that her only child would willingly choose to live so far away from us. She cried endlessly upon his leaving home, and she fretted daily—there were long phone calls and sporadic weekend visits—my son was very

good about humoring his poor worried mother, until his second semester away, that is.

The girl's name was Evelyn. She had met my son midway through
that first semester; they began dating very soon thereafter, and in a
very timely and surprisingly efficient fashion, she proceeded to de-
stroy our son piecemeal. Suddenly, the drive and the will that had
made him the young man that he was had disappeared altogether, his
grades suffered mightily, and his class attendance became intermittent
at best, before ultimately becoming sporadic. His mother at once sus-
pected drugs, but I myself knew better—my son was merely a victim
of circumstance, having fallen in love with the wrong type of woman.
And when this succubus finally broke it off with him, my once-strong
son became nothing more than a shell of his former self-assured self.
A semester later he had flunked out completely, lost his scholarships,
and was back at home with his mother and I. And I must admit, the
two of us together, despite our monumental disappointment, were
quite happy to have him back home again.

He still pined for her, of course—there were endless text mes-
sages, and late-night talks that morphed into heated arguments—but
very soon it was clear even to our own son that the siren had moved
on to other prey, another young man that my son knew in passing,
and secretly, despite the pain we knew it was causing our only child,
his mother and I couldn't have been happier at this new development.
And so, with the passing of time, after a few weeks of serious wound-
licking and navel-gazing, my son picked himself back up off the
ground, rising like a phoenix through the flames of tribulation, and
he began to move on again with his life.

I insisted he come work for me. Mind you, he was not qualified
in any way, shape, or form, but he was more than intellectually capa-
ble, smarter, as it was, than his father, and, at the end of the day, there
are worse crimes for a man to commit than nepotism. Besides, it af-

forded me the opportunity to keep a wary eye on him and his development, and in time, he began to do a passable job. He made his mistakes, but nothing I could not correct or amend as I needed to, and eventually, he even began to smile and laugh again, and there was even more-than-idle talk of him taking some classes at the local community college in the spring, and once again, things were beginning to look Providential.

But, as we have all seen from time to time, Providence has a wicked way of shifting gears and changing course suddenly and without warning.

The Universe always has a way of balancing itself back out again.

The last Sunday I ever saw my son alive began as any other Sunday during the late fall. It was football season, of course, football being considered religion in Texas, and my son, my wife, and I were preparing to watch the Cowboys game. My son, being the good, helpful young man that he was, had volunteered to go to the store and acquire provisions, such as beer, ice, chips, and so on, to be consumed during the game. So, he borrowed his mother's car and left for the store, and his mother and I waited patiently for his safe return, as all parents do . . .

. . . he came tearing back into the house in a frightful panic not twenty minutes later, sans the provisions, and he proceeded to frantically spin a story so preposterous—so unbelievable—that I knew at once it had to be true, for such a story simply could not be made up.

He had been at the store, my son said excitedly, waiting in the checkout line, when none other than Death Herself had come into the store. (How he knew She was Death my son did not say, and I did not interrupt his hysterical ramblings to ask, but I instinctively knew, as I am quite sure my wife did as well, that when one lays their eyes upon Death, one knows.) They made eye-contact, my son said, and Death beckoned toward him. Terrified, he left the cart in the checkout line and ran out of the store as fast as he could run.

"I need the truck!" my son fairly shrieked at me. "I must go to Grandma's house in Houston; there, amongst the throngs of people in the big city, Death will never know where to find me!" Of course, his mother and I agreed with him, and the arrangements were made quickly; our son was on his way to Houston in a matter of minutes.

My wife was understandably very upset by the whole scene, but I, being of the age that I was and not so much afraid of Death anymore, took it upon myself to drive my wife's car back to the store with the purpose of confronting Death over the matter—it had to have been a simple misunderstanding, I reasoned. Upon arriving at the store, I did not have to look hard for Death; I found Her there in the frozen food section, closely following behind an elderly couple who did not seem to be aware of Her there.

"There you are! How dare you frighten my son!" I exclaimed, pointing an aged-yet-purposeful finger at Her. "He's a good boy, our only child, and he is far too young to die! If you must, on this day, take a Cunningham, take me instead, and leave my boy be!"

Death smiled wanly at me, Her tone even and placid when She spoke. "I admire your courage and your noble attempt at sacrifice, but I assure you, it was not my intention to frighten your son; I was merely surprised to see him here in such a small town. You see, I have an appointment with him tonight in Houston."